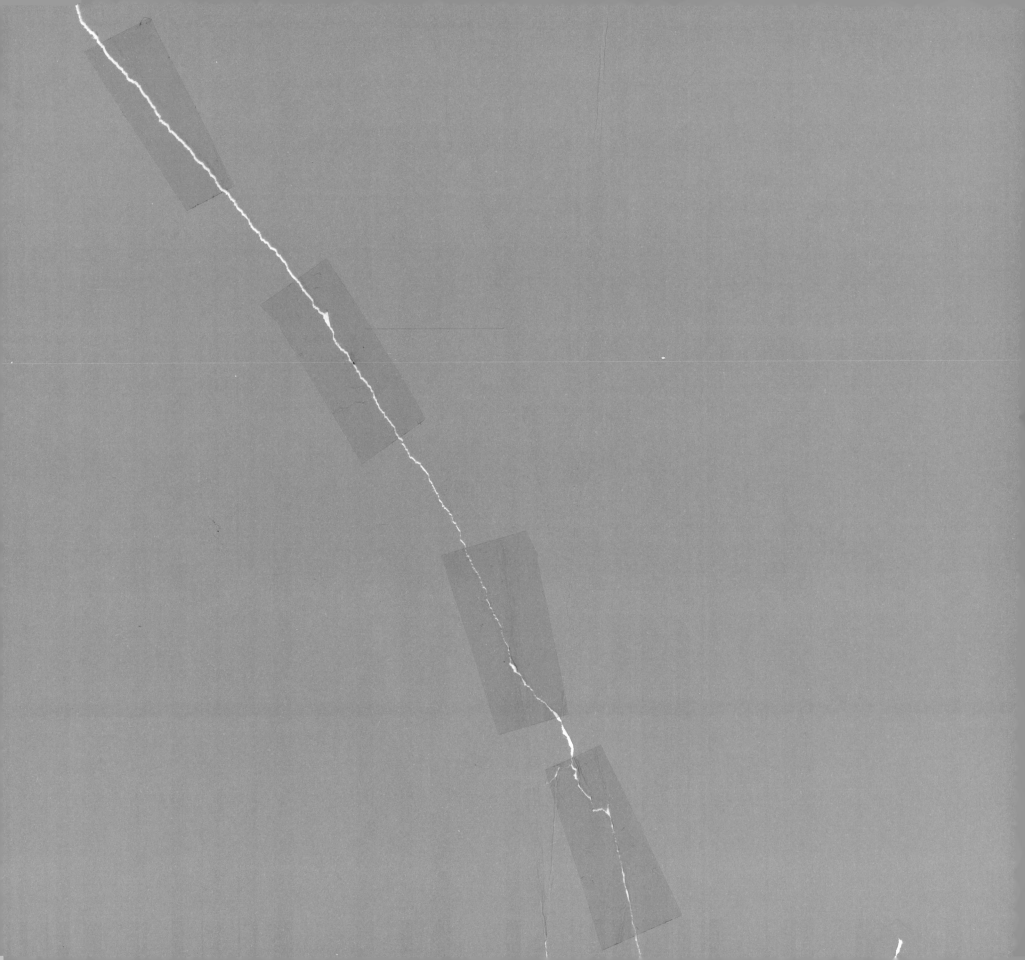

BABIES ON THE GO

Linda Ashman   ILLUSTRATED BY Jane Dyer

HARCOURT, INC.
Orlando   Austin   New York   San Diego   London

Library of Congress Cataloging-in-Publication Data
Ashman, Linda.
Babies on the go/Linda Ashman; illustrated by Jane Dyer.
p. cm.
Summary: Illustrations and rhyming text show how different animals carry their babies when they are on the move.
1. Parental behavior in animals—Juvenile literature.   2. Animals—Infancy—Juvenile literature.   3. Animal locomotion—Juvenile literature.
[1. Parental behavior in animals.   2. Animals—Infancy.   3. Animal locomotion.]   I. Dyer, Jane.   II. Title.
QL762.A84   2003
591.56'3—dc21   2002006310
ISBN 978-0-15-201894-8

LEO   10 9 8 7 6 5 4

4500328273

Printed in China

The illustrations in this book were done in Winsor & Newton watercolors
on Arches 140 lb. hot-press watercolor paper.
The display type was hand lettered by Georgia Deaver.
The text type was set in Diotima.
Color separations by Bright Arts Ltd., Hong Kong
Printed and bound by LEO, China
Production supervision by Sandra Grebenar and Ginger Boyer
Designed by Judythe Sieck

For Uncle Arthur and Aunt Jackie, with love—*L. A.*

For my friends Eric and Bobbie Carle—*J. D.*

Some babies stand up right away.

They take a step, then run and play.

But many need more time to grow,

so they have *other* ways to go....

Rolling by in baby strollers.

Holding tight to Mother's shoulders.

Grabbing on to clumps of hair.

Riding bareback through the air.

Swinging in a belly sling.

Sailing snug beneath a wing.

Towed along a bumpy trail.

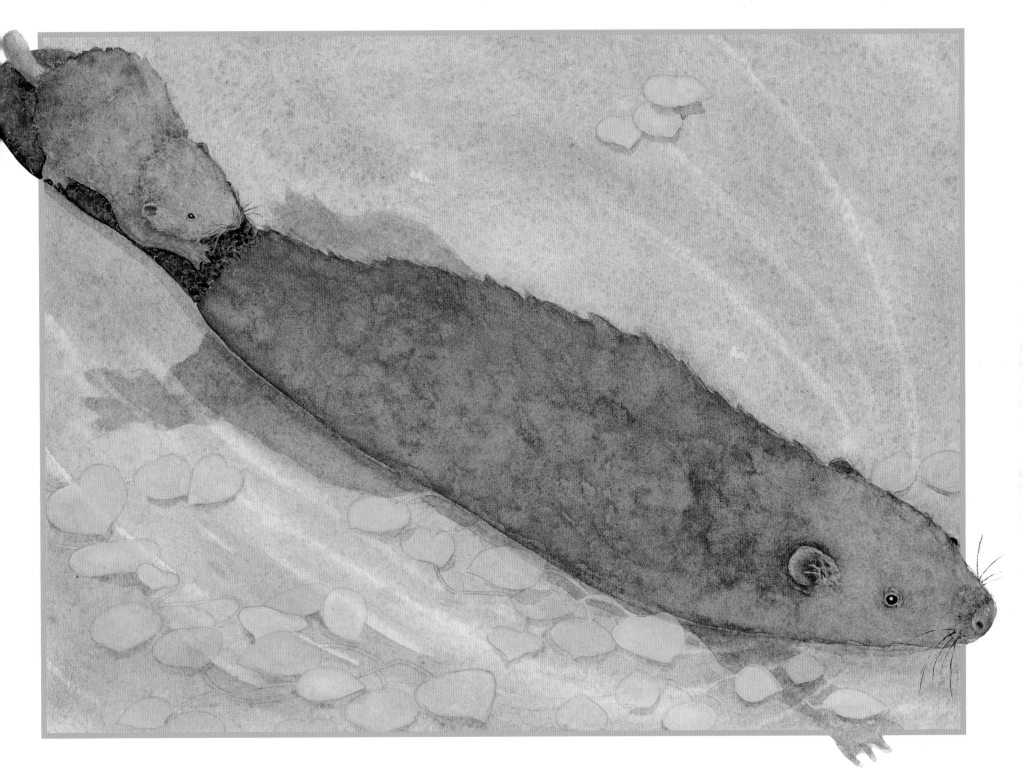

Surfing on a paddle-tail.

Flying by beneath a cape.

Dangling from a fuzzy nape.

Nudged along with gentle paws.

Floating by in giant jaws.

Perching on a mother's hip.

Stretching out on board a ship.

Tucked inside a private sack.

Boosted by a piggyback.

Touring solo on their ride.

Squeezed together, side by side.

It doesn't matter how they go.

Inside...outside...fast...or slow.

On the ground

or high above,

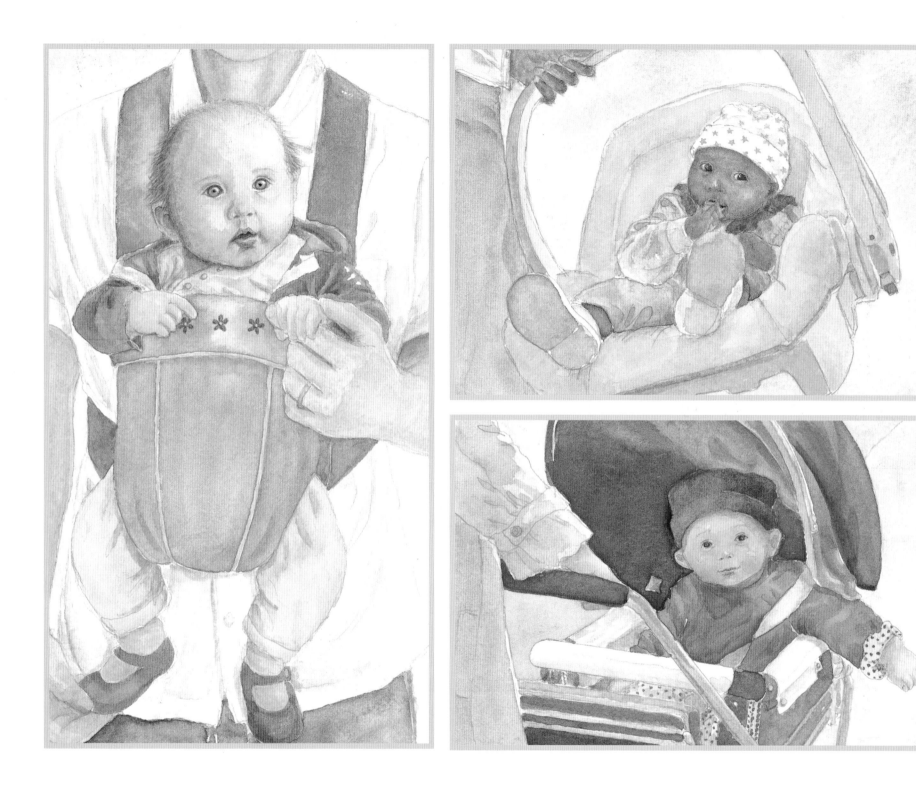

babies always ride with love.

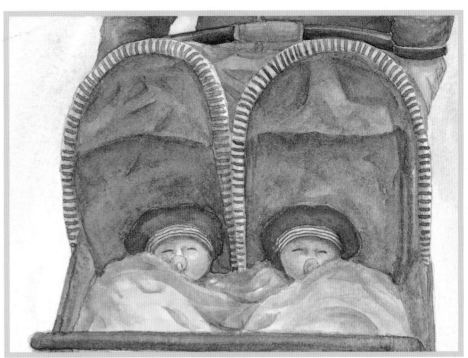
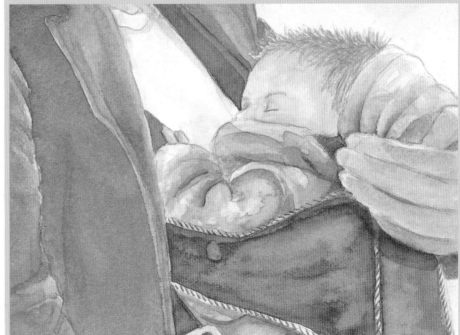

Meet the Babies

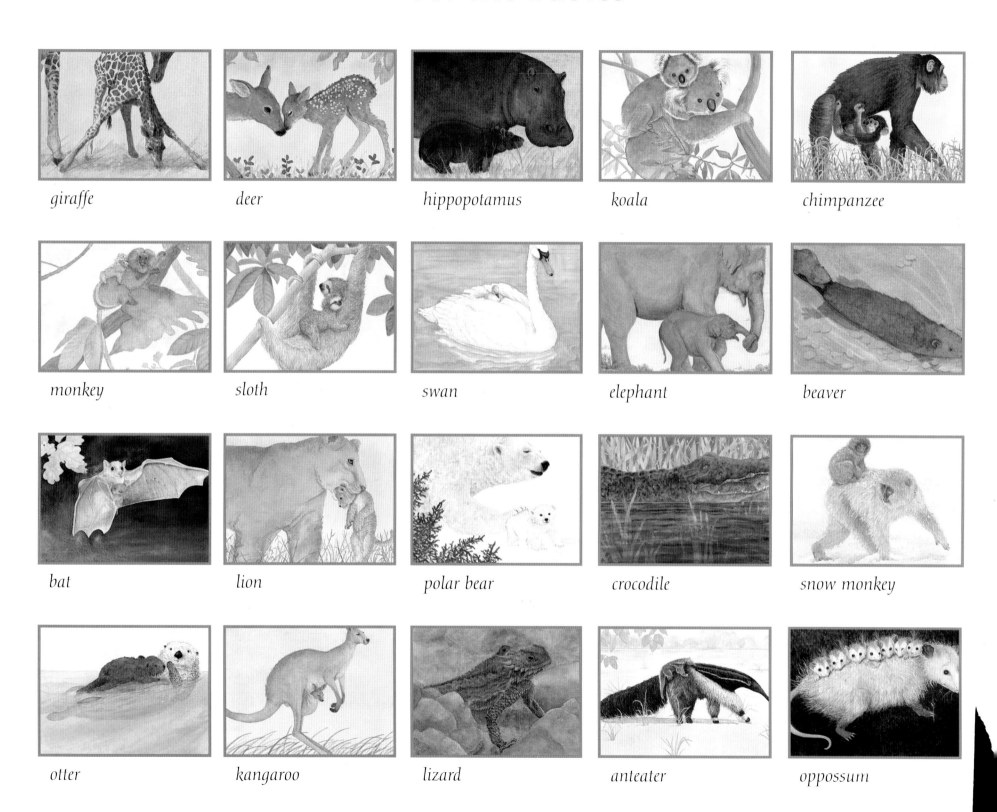

giraffe

deer

hippopotamus

koala

chimpanzee

monkey

sloth

swan

elephant

beaver

bat

lion

polar bear

crocodile

snow monkey

otter

kangaroo

lizard

anteater

oppossum